Ayla Bayla

A Book by David Harold

ISBN-13: 978-0991344505
ISBN-10: 0991344502

Published by Schwierd Books, an imprint of Blue House / Magoo. For information about special discounts and bulk purchases please visit: www.schwierdbooks.com, or contact us by e-mail: books@schwierdbooks.com. Contact the author: dave@schwierdbooks.com

Schwierd Books

An imprint of
Blue House / Magoo

Ayla Bayla

The first book of

The Ayla Bayla Book Collection

A book by David Harold

Schwierd Books

For

My nieces and nephews, with love.

The world is a better place with these five

living, laughing and loving in it.

Table of Contents

CHAPTER 1 The Mysterious It 1

CHAPTER 2 A Noteworthy Note 11

CHAPTER 3 Unusual Classmates, Unusual Class 18

CHAPTER 4 Does *It* Exist? 28

CHAPTER 5 A Terrifying Discovery 36

CHAPTER 6 You Want Me To Do *What*? 43

CHAPTER 7 Sneaking Around 48

CHAPTER 8 A Past Conflict Revealed 56

CHAPTER 9 Caught! 65

CHAPTER 10 The Show Must Go On! 76

CHAPTER 11 "It's Not Fair!" 82

CHAPTER 12 Unexpected Honor 87

CHAPTER 13 A Change of Heart 90

CHAPTER 1

The Mysterious It

"Pull!"

Ricky Spears held its arms. Ahmed Patel held its legs.

"Pull harder!"

Between them, the chubby baby twisted and wriggled.

"Wait a minute." Ricky let go of the arms and grabbed the head. "Now pull!"

The boys tugged and *Bok!* the head came right off.

"You killed my baby!" Jenny Adams screamed.

Ricky held the head in his hands. Ahmed held the body upside down by its legs. It looked like a

Thanksgiving turkey.

They hadn't actually *killed* the baby, since it wasn't alive to begin with. But without doubt, Ricky and Ahmed had injured Jenny's *Chubs-N-Hugs* doll beyond repair.

"I just got her for my birthday!" Jenny sobbed as the older boys went back to tugging at the baby's arms and legs. "Now she's dead!"

The headless baby looked like a football, which is exactly what the boys wanted. Their game had come to a screeching halt when Skeeter Gulikson accidentally threw the real ball into the creek. They needed a new one, and Jenny and her baby doll just happened to be nearby.

The other older boys waited impatiently as Ahmed and Ricky struggled to pull off the arms and legs.

"Would you two hurry up? The school bell is going to ring!" a boy said.

"I know!" Ricky shot back. "But the dang things won't come off!"

* * *

Hi! My name is Ayla.

Ayla Bayla.

I'm a regular girl. I live on a regular street, in a regular house.

My dad just dropped me off for school.

There he goes! You can still wave to him if you want.

I have lots of friends here at school. Wherever I go, I seem to make friends with everyone.

Well, everyone except the mean older boys who just broke Jenny's doll.

I don't like them at all.

* * *

Standing nearby, I scratched my middle fingernail on the second button of my coat (a habit I've had since I was a baby). I was unable to stand Jenny's wailing any longer.

I whispered something to Juanita Wilson

standing next to me and she nodded.

"Good idea," she said.

She turned to the mean older boys: "I'm going to tell a teacher you broke Jenny's doll!"

Ricky saw it was my idea and shot me a mean look. "Ayla! Why don't you stay out of this and go back to your class of weirdos!"

Jaunita taunted: "Boys...I'm leaving now..."

Ricky scowled and quickly shoved the headless baby body into Jenny's arms, but he scooped up the head and ran away. He told the boys to find sticks so they could play hockey with it.

I patted Jenny on the shoulder. "It's ok," I told her. "You still have most of her."

Jenny's nostrils flared. "But that's no good! How's she going to eat?"

"Well, that *is* a problem."

But it was Jenny's problem. Besides, Jaunita was heading toward the teacher, so I was sure justice would be done soon enough.

I left the scene and skipped away toward the monkey bars—my favorite piece of playground equipment.

"Hey, Ayla!" Jimmy Sneezywitz called out.

"Hey, Jimmy! What are you doing?"

"Playing a game of hopscotch. We need two more."

I walked over and couldn't help but ask, "Has anyone seen *it* lately?"

Ellen Sunnyside nearly fainted.

"No," Sally Trapsaddle replied, unfazed. "And I hope I never see *it* anytime soon. I don't even believe *it* exists, but even if *it* does, which I know *it* doesn't…"

"Charlie Reshbottom said he touched *it*!" Jimmy blurted.

"No way!" Ellen Sunnyside said.

"No way!" someone else said.

Sally Trapsaddle gagged. "He *touched it*? Ewwwww!"

"That's silly," I butted in. "No one's ever touched *it*."

"How do you know?" Jimmy retorted.

"Because how could anyone ever get close enough to touch *it*?"

"Oooooooooooo," Chunky Cabunky piped-in cheerfully. "I wonder what *it* felt like?"

Chunky is my best friend, but ewww, what happened to her face?

"What happened to your face?"

"I flew off the swing set and landed on my cheek! But as my face was grinding through the gravel, I looked up and saw how deep the blue sky was, and how beautiful it looked on such a nice day as this. I also heard a bird singing and saw some colorful flowers as I slid to a stop near the monkey bars..."

Good old Chunky. Nothing ever gets her down. She's always positive. Always cheerful.

Chunky's full name is Chunky Chocolate Chip Cabunky. Her parents named her after their favorite ice cream: Chunky Chocolate Chip. Isn't that funny? I think so. But she doesn't eat a whole lot of ice cream. She actually doesn't like sweets. She's skinny as a rail. Isn't that weird? I think so.

"Ayla, quit yappin'! We're in the middle of a game," Jimmy scolded.

Sally Trapsaddle was in the middle of her turn. She picked up her rock and hopped and dribbled back to 'start' on her third lap up and back.

"Ten, Seven..."

Rudi Bhat threw a ball at her but missed.

We don't play hopscotch the normal way. We play our own version, with made-up rules and teams and everything.

Our rules are that you have to go back and forth three times instead of once, and you have to bounce a basketball the whole time.

Sound hard? It is! But it's fun!

Oh, I forgot another rule: A person from the other team gets one chance to hit you with a volleyball from twenty feet away while you're skipping.

If they hit you, you're out.

"...Five, Two, Done!" Sally yelped.

Ellen Sunnyside was livid. "No fair! On number seven she stepped on the line! That doesn't count!"

"Yeah!" someone said.

"Yeah!" someone else said.

"No, I didn't!" Sally protested. "I went like this." And Sally walked back to number seven and stomped down hard on it with both feet.

"Nuh uh!" someone said.

"Nuh uh!" someone else said.

"You didn't do it like that!" Jimmy retorted.

That's my other best friend, Jimmy Sneezywitz.

Jimmy is the opposite of Chunky. He can't say anything good, just like Chunky can't say anything bad. Jimmy thinks the worst of every situation. Like when we rode the roller coaster at the amusement park. Afterwards, all Jimmy could say was, "It was too windy and it gave me an upset stomach."

"Ooh!" Chunky offered: "Let's go on the Tilt-O-Whirl and see if you throw up!"

Yes, Jimmy takes a little getting used to, but he's a good guy. Someday Chunky's cheerfulness might rub off on him.

At least, I'm hoping it does.

Everyone continued arguing about the game, but my brain was stuck on something so mysterious, so *horrible*, having to do with this unknown thing rumored to be roaming our school hallways this year. The mysterious *it*.

A mystery I was dead set to get to the bottom of...

Brrriiinnnngggggg!

Oh! The school bell! Time to get to class!

"Hey guys," I said to Jimmy and Chunky, "I have to drop off a note at the office. It's from my mom. Will you tell Mrs. Bleeblebrom I'll be late?"

"Sure!" Chunky said cheerfully.

"Whatever," Jimmy sighed.

"Bye Chunky!"

"Bye Ayla!"

"Bye Jimmy!"

"Whatever."

"Don't let *it* get you," I called to them.

Chunky chuckled.

Jimmy gagged.

* * *

Chunky, Jimmy and I go to Skeeziks Elementary

School. It's my fourth grade year. Jimmy's a year older than us, but we're still in the same class, isn't that weird? We've only been in school a couple months now, but we're halfway to Christmas break. I always count the days until Christmas because Christmas is my favorite holiday. And because we get a lot of days off school.

Well, here I am at the office. It always smells weird in here.

Hey! There's a new kid over there waiting to see the principal. I wonder if he'll be in our class? I don't see anyone behind the counter. I'll just toss the note up there.

(CRASH!)

What was that? Did you hear that? I hope it isn't what I think it is, but I'm not staying around to find out!

Bye!

CHAPTER 2

A Noteworthy Note

I slumped down at my desk.

Oh! I forgot to tell you. Mrs. Bleeblebrom is my teacher. She's a good teacher. You'd like her.

Do you want to know a secret about Mrs. Bleeblebrom you probably don't know? She has really big hands. But she has a normal size head. Her hands are big and puffy, like boxing gloves. We're all scared of that, because Carl Poopenhott got a good grade on a test once, and Mrs. Bleeblebrom gave him a 'Good job!' whack on the back. It left a big, red blotch on his back for *three weeks*!

I really like our classroom. You would too. We have computers, and weird science stuff, and everything.

Oh, and you know what? We have this huge TV screen in our classroom where the chalkboard used to be. I think it's called a plastic TV...or maybe plasm...or plasma...oh, that's it! Plasma! (I think plasma is another word for blood, but I'm not sure, and that's gross anyway.)

So what's so great about the giant TV in the front of the room? It's because our desks have a special surface so that when you write on top of it, it shows on the screen in the front. Isn't that cool? No more embarrassing walks to the front of the classroom.

Mrs. Bleeblebrom suddenly clapped her big hands to bring us to attention. "Class, we'll now begin our lesson on language. Who would like to volunteer to tell us the silliest words they've ever heard?"

While she said this, I leaned over to Chunky and whispered, "I saw *it*."

"You what?" she whispered back.

"Ayla!" Mrs. Bleeblebrom called from the front of the room.

I gulped. "Yes, Mrs. Bleeblebrom?"

"Can you give me an answer to my question?"

"Uh, yeah. The silliest word I've ever heard is 'eggnog.'"

I giggled a little.

"Ew," someone said.

"Ok, please spell that for us on your desk," Mrs. Bleeblebrom said.

I wrote E G G N O G on my desk and it showed on the screen at the front of the room.

"Very good," Mrs. Bleeblebrom encouraged. "Anyone else?"

Chunky raised her hand. "Chicken gizzards!'"

"Ewwwww!" a few kids shrieked.

"Ok, Chunky. Please spell that," Mrs. Bleeblebrom instructed.

Chunky wrote C H I C K E N L I Z Z A R D S and everyone laughed—even Chunky—though she didn't know why.

Mrs. Bleeblebrom clapped her big hands. "Ok, that's enough children." She walked over and erased the 'L' on Chunky's desk and wrote 'G.'

She looked up at the class. "Anyone else?"

"I feel bloated," Jimmy blurted.

"EWWWWWWWW!" everyone screamed, but he really did feel bloated.

"Please write it."

Jimmy wrote I FEEL BOATED and everyone laughed. Then he leaned forward and vomited all over the floor.

"EWWWW!" everyone screamed as Jimmy ran out of the room.

"Jackson," Mrs. Bleeblebrom said to a boy near the front, "could you please go find the janitor and ask him to clean that up?"

Jackson nodded and left the room.

"What about you Mrs. Bleeblebrom?" I asked. "What's the silliest words *you've* ever heard?"

"Yeah!" the class urged.

"No, I don't have to do it. I'm the teacher."

"Come on, *please*?"

"Ok. The silliest words I ever heard were 'you should go into teaching.'"

"Ewwww...huh?"

Just then, a knock at the door startled us all. We

figured it was Jackson coming back with the janitor, but it was actually a messenger from the office. He handed Mrs. Bleeblebrom a note. She thanked him, closed the door and sat at her desk.

"Children, please work quietly a moment while I read this."

As Mrs. Bleeblebrom scanned the note, a worried look crept across her face. I watched from my seat in the back of the room, hoping she was ok. I couldn't really see anything, but wished it wasn't anything bad. I really don't like bad things, because once there was this time when...

"Ayla!" Chunky whispered loudly from the desk next to me.

I nearly jumped out of my seat. "*What*?"

"Shhhhhhhhhh," Mrs. Bleeblebrom shushed, without looking up from the note.

"The door!" Chunky whispered tersely.

I looked at the door. It was slightly ajar.

"Something dark passed by," Chunky said quietly. "And it made a strange sound."

"I didn't hear anything."

"That's because you were daydreaming, silly!"

"Oh, yeah. Well, what kind of sound did it make?"

"A slithering sound. A slithering, sluthering, slothering sound," Chunky blathered like a blithering fool.

"Ewwwww!" I said. I couldn't believe I didn't hear it, but then again I was more focused on Mrs. Bleeblebrom and her note.

And that worried look on her face.

"Oh my goodness," Mrs. Bleeblebrom said quietly to herself. I was the only one that heard it, since I was the only one watching her.

Mrs. Bleeblebrom looked up from the note. "He's really done it this time!"

Everyone stopped what they were doing.

"What's the matter, Mrs. Bleeblebrom?" I asked. "What happened?"

She stood up. "I can't speak about it now children. But we'll talk about it tomorrow, after I've had some time to think. Class is dismissed for recess."

Everyone rushed from the room, trying to step

carefully around Jimmy's vomit. But the sight and smell was too much for some, and they gagged and several threw up right in the same spot.

Mrs. Bleeblebrom sighed and buried her face in her big glove-hands.

CHAPTER 3

Unusual Classmates, Unusual Class

Recess! And it's a beautiful day outside!

"This weather is a drag," Jimmy mourned. "The sun is too shiny and it's too warm for me to wear my new jacket."

"I love the sun," Chunky chirped. "The sun gives us warmth and light, which gives life to all the little animals. And it gives the plants the energy to grow and…"

"Ok already!" Jimmy scoffed.

Chunky smiled at him then turned to me. "So Ayla, you said you saw *it*?"

"Yeah, I think so. I was waiting at the counter in the office and I heard this huge crash and looked up and a side office door was open just a little bit and…"

"Jeez, take a breath," Jimmy interrupted.

"...and I looked and saw something moving quickly and..."

"What did it look like?" Chunky asked.

"Well, I couldn't see very well, but it looked really dark."

"Ooooooooh," my friends gasped.

Just then, a little boy walked up.

"Hi!" the little boy greeted us.

"Hi!" Chunky said. "My name's Chunky! What's your name?"

"Hi Chunky!" the boy said. "Your name is funky. My name is Clay Brown. This is a great playground."

"You talk kind of funny," Chunky observed.

"Yes, I know. But don't go. I've been this way for a long time. Seems I always have to rhyme."

"Are you the new kid?" I asked.

"I sure am. Yesterday I swam. I went to the pool and didn't break a rule."

"Uh, that's nice," I said, sort of confused. "Well, I guess you'll fit right in with us. This is Chunky. She can't say anything bad. And this is Jimmy. He can't say anything good. My name is Ayla Bayla. I'm just a regular girl."

"Hi, Chunky," the boy said again. "It's fun to watch a monkey. Hi, Jimmy. Giraffes are skinny."

"That's neat!" Chunky exclaimed excitedly.

"Whatever," Jimmy sighed.

Just then, the recess whistle blew.

"Well, it was nice to meet you all. After school we should go to the mall," Clay suggested.

"Welcome to our school, Clay," I told him.

"Thanks, Ayla Bayla. I like your name-a."

"I think I know why."

* * *

You might think Clay is strange, but I'm used to having quirky kids in my class.

Oh! I forgot to tell you. I'm actually not supposed to be in Mrs. Bleeblebrom's class. On the first day of school, I got mixed-up and went to the wrong classroom.

Mrs. Bleeblebrom didn't do roll-call first thing

that day like most teachers do. Instead she stood before the class and said, "Children, we have a new boy with us this year. Please say hi to Bob."

"Hi, Bob," the class greeted the boy, including me, since I thought I was in the right class.

"Lla uoy teem ot ecin," Bob answered.

"What?" everyone said at once, including Mrs. Bleeblebrom.

"He said, 'Nice to meet you all'," I told them.

Mrs. Bleeblebrom looked at me in surprise. "You understood what he said?"

"Well, yes." It wasn't hard, I thought. The boy just spoke everything backwards.

Mrs. Bleeblebrom approached my desk. "And what is your name, young lady?"

"Ayla. Ayla Bayla."

"Well, Miss Bayla, I need to ask Bob a few questions but can't understand a word he's saying. If you don't mind, would you tell me what he says?"

Mrs. Bleeblebrom asked the questions, Bob answered, and this is what I told the class:

"Bob's full name is Clarence Slim-Bob Nipper-

Cakes. His mother, Mary Nipper, and his father, Eugene Cakes, met at a pie eating contest. It's a very crazy and silly story. Bob said he would tell it later. Anyway, when his parents discovered Bob's strange way of speaking, they just called him Bob. I guess that was a good thing."

"Thank you, Miss Bayla," Mrs. Bleeblebrom interjected. "That'll be enough for now." She peered at me with a strange look. "And I'd like to see you after class today."

What? Am I in trouble? But what'd I do?

* * *

After school that first day, Mrs. Bleeblebrom put her gloves, er, uh, hands, on my shoulders. She looked me straight in the eye. "Miss Bayla, you're not supposed to be in my class."

"I'm not?" I answered weakly, kind of afraid.

"No, you're not. I noticed it right away. Of the twenty-five kids in my class, most have been here for two or three years now. I have many different grade levels in my class because, well, you see, my class is for kids who are...*different* than other kids."

"Different? How?"

"Well, let's see. Take for example the boy with the green skin who is covered with polka dots, or the girl who always brings her pet ant-eater to class. And then there's Reeker McBean. Oh, yes, good old Reeker McBean!"

"Reeker McBean?"

"Yes. Reeker McBean. The child has strange odors coming from him. And they change all the time. The moment I met him, he smelled like flowers. A few hours later he smelled like a skunk! Later on, he smelled like pineapples. The next day, I could have sworn he smelled just like dog poop!"

"Really?"

"Yes, really. And he talks in smells too."

"He does?"

"Yes. One day I asked him to describe a room in his house. He said, 'In my kitchen, there is a stove, a microwave, a refrigerator and a stink.' So I said, 'You mean a *sink*?, and he said, 'That's what I said, a stink.'"

"That's kind of funny."

"I thought so too, and so I asked him if he liked jokes. He said, 'Yes, I have a great sense of fume-er.'"

"Wow."

"Uh-huh. That's what I thought, too. So then I asked him what kind of job he wants to have when he grows up, and he said, 'I'm not sure what I want to do when I get odor.'"

"Hmm. That *is* different."

"And then there's Clara Bell. She speaks with animal noises."

"Really? That sounds pretty neat."

"Yes, to you and I it does, but in regular classrooms it can be pretty disruptive." Mrs. Bleeblebrom sat down at her desk and heaved a heavy sigh. "So you see, there's nothing wrong with these children, Ayla. They're just a bit...what shall I say?...different. And you will find in life that people out there in the world want everyone to be exactly like themselves. To have the same color skin, to talk the same way, to come from the same place, to like the same animals, to prefer the same flavor of pudding. And if they *don't*, people make fun of them and are mean to them."

"Yes, people can be very mean sometimes," I agreed.

"But what if everyone was exactly the same?" Mrs. Bleeblebrom said. "Can you imagine how boring *that* would be?"

"I like different kinds of people," I told her. "You know, this class sounds like a lot of fun. I'm glad I'm in it."

"Well, that's the problem. You aren't officially in my class right now. And I'm not sure if you'd be allowed to stay."

"*What*?" I shrieked. "But I want to stay with you, Mrs. Bleeblebrom! I like you. You're a good teacher."

"That's why I wanted to talk to you, Ayla. I'm going to ask the principal if you can stay in my class."

"You are? But I don't talk strange or have funny smells or anything...do I?"

"No, you don't. But I need you here because I

can't understand a word Clarence Slim-Bob Nipper-Cakes says, and you can. So I need your help."

"I'd be glad to help you Mrs. Bleeblebrom. I'm sure the principal will let me stay."

"You know we have a new principal this year, don't you?"

"No, I didn't."

"There might be big problems ahead for us this year."

"Big problems? Why?"

"Because the new principal and I were in college together many years ago. And I'm afraid he doesn't like me very much."

"You? How could anyone not like *you*? You're so nice."

"Well, what happened between him and me is a story for another time. So go on home now. I'll see you in class tomorrow."

* * *

It turned out, the new principal did let me stay

in Mrs. Bleeblebrom's class, much to my delight.

And that is how I met Chunky and Jimmy and all the others.

And that is how Mrs. Bleeblebrom and I began a great friendship.

And that is how I'd come to face the most difficult challenge of my life so far.

CHAPTER 4

Does *It* Exist?

Ok, let's come back to today.

Remember? Recess had just ended and we all went back to class.

"Children, listen up," Mrs. Bleeblebrom said. "Before we do our math lesson, I want to introduce a new student. Please say hello to Clay Brown."

"Hello, Clay," the class said.

"Hey! It's a beautiful day," Clay responded.

"Children, please open your math books to page nine. Clay…"

"Yes ma'am? I'd like some ham."

Everyone giggled.

"Um, well, uh, ok, I'm sorry, I don't have any ham right now, son, but could you please tell us what

7 plus 8 equals?"

"The answer is fifteen. Some people don't have a spleen."

"Yes, well, Clay that's very nice," Mrs. Bleeblebrom replied. "And yes, the answer is fifteen. Good job. Now can you write that for us on your desk?"

Clay wrote: $7 + 8 = 15$ S O M E P E O P L E D O N ' T H A V E A S P L E E N.

Mrs. Bleeblebrom sighed. "Uh, yes. That is correct, Clay."

Clay sat back with a huge smile.

We did math for the rest of the morning until Mrs. Bleeblebrom dismissed us for lunch.

* * *

At lunch, Jimmy, Chunky and I usually sat with the Bunson twins, Emmitt and Nolan. They're fifth graders and everyone thinks they're the coolest kids in school. They drive their own monster trucks to school. Can you believe that? They really do. I'm not joking.

Emmitt plays football and Nolan plays baseball. They play jokes on people whenever they can. It can be annoying, but most of the time they make me laugh.

"Hey Jimmy," I said. "I'm really thirsty. Are you going to drink your milk?"

"No, I don't think so. It's green and smells like rotten eggs. I think it's spoiled. You want it?"

"I don't want it *that* bad." I scrunched my nose in an *eww* kind of way. I looked at Chunky. "Hey Chunky, are you going to drink your milk?"

"Yes, indeed I am. Milk contains nutrients and vitamins to make one grow up and have strong bones, which helps us stay in great shape to become the best people we can possibly be."

"Oh, brother," Jimmy sighed.

I changed the subject. "Mrs. Bleeblebrom looked really scared today when she read that note."

"What note?" Nolan asked.

"Someone from the office brought her a note," I told him.

"Maybe the note was about *it*?" Emmitt offered.

"What *it*?" Nolan asked.

"You know…*it*. *It*." Emmitt urged.

"Oh, hogwash," Nolan retorted. "There's no *it*. Someone just made that up."

"No, it's real," Chunky jumped in. "I saw something weird today. I think it was part of *it*. I heard *it*, too."

I added, "Yeah, and I heard a crash in the office and saw something dark moving behind the desk."

"Well, if there is an *it* around here," Nolan said confidently, "Emmitt and I will find *it*. You can bet on that."

"Yeah!" Emmitt agreed, and they high-fived each other.

All of a sudden, Nolan screamed, "Oh no! Emmitt! You just drank Jimmy's milk. I think he's gonna be sick!"

Emmitt gagged and milk sprayed out of his nose, splashing Reeker McBean, who sat one table away, across from the girl with the ant-eater.

Nolan and Emmitt laughed and slapped each other another high-five.

"You guys are gross," Jimmy said. Just then, a giant glob of chocolate pudding shot from the hand of Reeker McBean missed Emmitt's head by an inch and splashed across Jimmy's face.

SPLAT!

Jimmy scooped up the biggest handful of creamed corn you've ever seen and threw it right back at Reeker. Some of it hit Reeker. Some of it hit the girl with the ant-eater. But most of it hit the ant-eater. Right on the nose.

And right *in* the nose.

The startled ant-eater leaned back and waved its nose in the air as if it couldn't breathe. Then it slammed its paws on the table and sneezed the most horrific sneeze in the history of the Skeeziks Elementary School cafeteria.

With the sound of a thousand trumpets, pellets of creamed corn shot into every corner of the lunchroom. No one escaped the creamed corn explosion, especially not the boy with the green skin and polka dots, who happened to be sitting right next to the ant-eater.

"I hate creamed corn!" the boy yelped, and left the lunchroom.

On her way into the cafeteria, Mrs. Bleeblebrom slid through a slick of chocolate pudding and fell right on her rump!

Everyone laughed hysterically.

"Oh, my goodness!" Mrs. Bleeblebrom exclaimed from flat on her back.

Helga the lunch lady laughed so hard she knocked over the giant container of grape drink. Eggy Peterson sprang up on the serving table just as the river of grape drink gushed toward his brand-new white sneakers. But instead of jumping *on* the table, Eggy missed it entirely and caught the edge of a tray of hot dogs, launching hundreds of wiener missiles throughout the room.

Carrie and Ruth Ann Peterbottom screamed and ran for cover, but not before *Pa-Pow, Pa-Pow, Pa-Pow!* three hot dogs slapped them across the face, sending them sprawling to the ground.

Near the exit, Kirk Carboodle stood laughing next to Daphne Doowainy (his one true puppy-love) but buckled over as he was also blasted in the face by a rogue wiener.

"I've been hit!" Kirk called out dramatically. "I'm going down! Don't worry about me, Daphne, save yourself!"

A startled Daphne hurried out of the cafeteria, leaving behind a wounded Kirk, hot dog slime dripping off both his cheeks.

I guess Kirk was not Daphne's one true puppy-love.

* * *

After the lunchroom riot, the rest of the day was pretty normal. Nothing really to tell.

But at home in bed that night, I couldn't sleep. I lay awake most of the night unable to stop my brain from working overtime.

What was the note to Mrs. Bleeblebrom about?

Would Emmitt and Nolan ever find out what *it*

is?

I picked a nugget of creamed corn out of my hair and finally rolled over and fell asleep.

CHAPTER 5

A Terrifying Discovery

The next day at school, I saw Chunky and Jimmy in the hallway before class.

"Hi, Ayla!" Chunky said. "Peace, love and happiness to you!"

"Hi, Chunky. Hi Jimmy."

Jimmy looked down. "Hey Chunky, your shoe is untied. You're going to trip and fall and break your arm. And it looks like someone put gum in your hair again."

Chunky grabbed a gob of goo from her 'do. "So they did. And it's my favorite flavor too!"

Across the hall, I saw Clara Bell bent over the drinking fountain trying to get a drink, but some mean older boy pushed her away.

"Get out of the way, bell dinger!" he said.

Clara looked up and spit water all over him.

"*MOOOOO* do you think you are?!" Clara yelled.

The other boys made fun of the mean boy and he ran away.

Clara is so cool, standing up for herself like that, I thought.

"We better get to class," I said to Chunky and Jimmy.

* * *

"Children, please take your seats and be quiet," Mrs. Bleeblebrom said. "We have a problem. A really big problem."

"Psssst..."

"I want you all to know that I believe in you. Every one of you..."

"Psssssst!"

I tried to pay attention, but I thought I heard a noise from the direction of the door.

"...and we'll get through this as best we can..."

our teacher continued.

"Ayla," came a weak whisper from the door.

Emmitt and Nolan were outside the door. And they looked scared! They were waving and pointing frantically down the hallway.

Again, I turned back and tried to pay attention to Mrs. Bleeblebrom, but Emmitt and Nolan seemed really worried.

I whispered harshly to the twins, "Go away! Mrs. Bleeblebrom will see you!"

But they didn't hear me. They were looking down the hall again.

Suddenly, they looked terrified!

I looked back at Mrs. Bleeblebrom.

"...what I need to tell you is nothing to be alarmed about..."

I looked again at the door.

Emmitt and Nolan were gone! What were they trying to tell me?

"...but some of you might find this scary. Very scary. Terrifying even," Mrs. Bleeblebrom continued.

What's that sound? It can't be!

Slithering?

All of a sudden, the door flew open. I nearly jumped out of my chair!

"...but children," Mrs. Bleeblebrom said, "Before we get to that, I want you to meet..."

With a loud sucking sound, a black shape slid into the room. It took two steps and crashed into an empty desk in the front row.

BANG!

"AAAAAHHHHH!" everyone screamed at once.

"...our new principal, Mr. Ray Cranklebucket," Mrs. Bleeblebrom announced.

Everyone's hair stood straight up (at least those who had hair).

Some ran. Some tried to jump out the window. Most wept silently at their desks.

Picking himself up off the floor, Principal Cranklebucket slurped, "Helllooooooo cheeeel-drin!"

He wore a black rain hat, a black raincoat, and black rubber boots. The black teeth in his mouth contained one very long, scraggly front tooth.

Ewww.

I looked down and saw that one foot was twice as long as the other. That's why he tripped and fell into the desk when he came in. He didn't seem to step with the long foot as much as he dragged it beside him, limping on the other leg, hunched as he walked.

But most interesting and most puzzling of all was this: he was dripping wet...though it hadn't rained all day.

"Get back in your seats," he screeched. "Now!"

Kids ran to their seats from all directions, many smashing into each other and falling down.

The principal impatiently tapped his long foot. A drop of water rolled from his forehead down his nose, until it dangled from the very tip of that one, very long, very scraggly, black tooth.

I looked outside. The sun was still shining. No rain today.

Mrs. Bleeblebrom said, "Children, Mr. Cranklebucket has chosen our class to perform the annual school play this year. We will perform the play three weeks from tonight for the entire school."

"Noooooooooooo!" the class shouted in horror, except for Chunky, who shouted "Hooray!"

"How will we do that?" asked Jimmy. "Most of us can't speak too well, and..."

"You will do as you're told!" Mr. Cranklebucket roared, blowing Jimmy's hair straight back. "And it better be better than last year's play! Even though I did hear excellent things about *How Larry Lizard Lips and Corina Crows Toes saved the U.S. Navy*."

"Yes, it was outstanding," Mrs. Bleeblebrom piped.

"Silence, you!" Principal Cranklebucket shrieked at her, blowing Mrs. Bleeblebrom's hair straight back. Then he turned and looked at us. "Good day, cheeeld-ren! And good luck. You're going to need it! Ha!" And he slithered toward the door.

Chunky was right. He sluthered, too.

Before reaching the door, the strange man turned and bellowed, "And good day to you, Mrs. Bleeble-BROOM! Ha ha ha ha ha ha!"

He slid through the door. It slammed shut behind him though he hadn't even touched it.

41

Omigosh! I thought. Emmitt and Nolan!

They were out in the hallway before Principal Cranklebucket came in, but now they were gone.

Disappeared!

CHAPTER 6

You Want Me To Do *What*?

I sat at my desk, nervous and scared:

I wonder if Emmitt and Nolan are all right?

I wonder how we can do a school play?

I wonder if they're serving creamed corn for lunch again today?

I walked to the front of the classroom, trying to muster some courage. "Come on you guys! We can do this play. People have been mean to you your whole lives, but that has made you stronger! I've seen you be brave and courageous. Like today, you Clara, at the drinking fountain."

"Thank you for *BRAAYING* that," Clara said, a little embarrassed and turning red.

"Let's show this school we're not afraid!" I

charged, then noticed Reeker McBean hiding under his desk.

Ummm...yeah.

Suddenly, the boy with the green skin and polka dots spoke up, "Ayla's right! We *can* do it!"

All the kids cheered.

"Ok, that settles it," I said, still standing in front of the class. "So what play should we put on? Any suggestions?"

"*Death of a Salesman*!" Jimmy suggested. "Or *Annie Get Your Gun*!"

"I think we should do *My Fair Lady*, Chunky said. "Or *The Sound of Music*!"

"It would be wise for us all," Clay suggested, "To do *Guys and Dolls*."

"How about *Ro-MEOW and Juliet*?" Clara offered.

"Nietsneknarf!" Bob blurted, but no one understood.

"Huh?" everyone asked.

"He said *Frankenstein*," I explained.

"Oh."

"We could do *Okl-aroma!*" Reeker spouted.

Mrs. Bleeblebrom had to stop the madness. "I have a better idea," she said as she stepped forward and put an arm around my shoulder. "Ayla, why don't *you* write our school play this year?"

"Really?" I said.

"Smeally?" Clay said.

"No!" Jimmy groaned.

"Yes!" Chunky cheered.

"Woc Yloh," Bob spat out, which no one understood.

"Heavens to *BARK*-sy!" Clara yelped.

"That's a gas!" Reeker added.

"Children, that'll be quite enough!" Mrs. Bleeblebrom scolded, clapping her gloves, er, I mean, her hands loudly. She dismissed the class for lunch.

"Mrs. Bleeblebrom!" I said sternly, "I want to see *you* after school." Then I left the room.

* * *

I went to the lunchroom, but was so angry I

didn't feel like eating anything.

"What's the matter Ayla?" Chunky asked cheerfully.

"I can't write a play. I've never written a play before," I sulked. "Why did Mrs. Bleeblebrom pick me? That was really mean of her. Besides, the whole school will make fun of us. Most kids in our class get made fun of all the time anyway. This will just make it worse. What could Mrs. Bleeblebrom be thinking?"

Just then, Nolan and Emmitt entered the lunchroom.

"Hey, are you two all right? What happened to you earlier?" I asked.

"We were on our way to gym class and saw *it*, or *him*, coming down the hallway to your classroom," Nolan explained. "We tried to warn you, but he got too close so we ran away."

"Yeah, we ran away," Emmitt repeated.

"Wow," Nolan continued, "That's one scary principal dude. There's something not quite right about that man."

"Yeah, I don't like the way he treated Mrs.

Bleeblebrom either." I remembered him snarling at her and making fun of her name.

"I think he's up to no good," Emmitt suggested.

"Yeah," Nolan said, looking at Emmitt. "We should keep an eye on him."

"Right," Emmitt nodded.

CHAPTER 7

Sneaking Around

I spoke with Mrs. Bleeblebrom after school that day.

"Mrs. Bleeblebrom, why did you pick me to write the school play? I've never done anything like that. I don't think I can."

She replied, "*You* may not think you can, but I *know* you can. Do you remember earlier in the school year when I had everyone write a short story?"

"Yes."

"Well, Chunky's story, *Everything is Bright and Beautiful* was pretty good. Jimmy's story, *The Day it Rained and Everyone's Toys Broke* might have been good, but I was too sad after reading it to care. Of course, I didn't understand a word of Bob's story. But your story, *Snarky Snarkles Snorkels in Scotland* was the best story I'd ever read from someone your age."

"Really?"

"Yes, and I know what it takes to write a good story. It's not easy."

"How do you know?"

"Because I'm not just a teacher. I'm a writer, too."

"You are?"

"Yes, and a really good one, if I do say so myself. But that was a long time ago, before I became a teacher."

"I don't think writing stories is very hard."

"That's because you have what is called 'talent.' Do you know what that means?"

"No."

"Talent means that you can do something better, or easier, than most other people because you were either born with a natural ability to do it, or you worked really hard to become good at it."

"Like Emmitt and Nolan playing sports?" I suggested.

"Yes, you could say they have a talent for

football and baseball."

"Does that mean they never have to practice?"

"Come here and look out the window," Mrs. Bleeblebrom motioned.

I saw Emmitt and Nolan tossing a football back and forth. I knocked on the window and waved to Emmitt. He looked at me right as Nolan threw the football. The ball slammed him in the side of the head, knocking him over.

"Whoops!" I said.

"See, they're practicing," Mrs. Bleeblebrom offered. "Practice and hard work is how you develop your talents."

"But how do I know what I have a talent for?"

"By working hard at everything you do. People around you will let you know what you're good at. Usually, you'll enjoy doing the things for which you have talent."

"What if I don't have any talent for anything?"

"Well, people can have many different talents, such as a talent for helping others, or making them feel better if they are sad, or a talent for making people laugh, or being able to understand and befriend people that others make fun of, or are mean to. Everyone has *some* talents."

I looked out the window and thought about what she was saying.

Then I saw *it*, now known as Principal Cranklebucket, scooting across the school parking lot. Emmitt and Nolan followed behind, hiding between cars so they wouldn't be seen.

"I'll do it, Mrs. B!" I said excitedly. "I'll work hard and we'll show that mean Principal Cranklebucket!"

"Hold on, Ayla," Mrs. Bleeblebrom stopped me and gently placed a glove, er, a hand, on my shoulder. "This won't be easy. But I want you to know that no matter what happens, as long as you've done your best, I'll be very proud of you."

"Thanks, Mrs. Bleeblebrom, I'll do my best. I promise."

* * *

The next day at recess we played our favorite game. It was called 'My Mama Said.'

Two people would swing a jump rope and you had to go the longest without messing up while everyone chanted a song.

I had a feeling Clay would love this game, because the songs always rhymed.

"I want to go first!" Chunky volunteered.

Jimmy and I swung the rope, and everyone sang:

"MY-MAMA-SAID-TO-TIE-YOUR-SHOE, TRY-NOT-TO-STEP-IN-DOGGY

"*DO*-THE-RIGHT-THING AND BE-A-MAN, DO-NOT-FORGET-TO-FLUSH-THE

"*CAN*-DY'S-YUMMY, CANDY'S-GREAT, PRIN-CIP-AL-C'S THE ONE-WE-HATE!"

Suddenly, a large rubber ball flew past me and struck Chunky in the head. She fell to the ground, scraping her knees and elbows.

"Omigosh!" I yelled, "Someone get the teacher!"

Bob ran to get her.

The teacher with recess duty that day was Mrs. Horsymouth. You wouldn't like her. She's mean. But that's her real name.

"What on earth is going on here?" Mrs. Horsymouth said. "I couldn't for the life of me understand a word this young child was trying to tell me."

"Chunky got hit in the head with a foul ball from the kick-ball game," I informed her.

"Well, let's have her not let it happen again," Mrs. Horsymouth said matter-of-factly.

"Uhhhhhh," Chunky moaned, laying on the ground.

"I think she's hurt real bad," I mentioned.

"Then take her to the nurse's office," Mrs. Horsymouth snapped, and walked away in a huff.

I told you she was mean.

"Jimmy, grab her legs," I instructed, and we carried her to the nurse's office.

We laid her on the cot and waited while Nurse Crumbcakes looked her over.

"Uuuhhhhh" Chunky moaned with her eyes

53

closed.

Nurse Crumbcakes lifted Chunky's eyelids one at a time and shined a little flashlight into her eyes.

"Well, she'll be all right, she just needs to rest here awhile," Nurse Crumbcakes said calmly.

"Can I stay with her?" I offered.

"Well, you'll miss the rest of recess, you know."

"I know, but I want to stay with her. That's ok by me."

Jimmy went back to recess and I sat and rubbed Chunky's shoulder while she lay there groaning.

Then she fell asleep.

I looked around the room, wondering what to do. I noticed a door in the back of the room, slightly ajar.

The teachers' lounge!

I looked in. No one was there. A jar of Tootsie Rolls sat on a counter across the room.

I love Tootsie Rolls!

I tiptoed quietly across the room. *Dink, Dink, Dink*...without warning, the hallway door burst open!

I dove behind a chair.

Mrs. Bleeblebrom and Mr. Gutsucker, the school janitor, entered the room.

Mrs. Bleeblebrom poured herself a cup of coffee. "Did you see that dancing show on TV last night?" she asked Mr. Gutsucker.

"Yeah, my wife makes me watch it all the time."

"Wasn't that a spectacular bright blue dress Tom Arnold was wearing?"

Suddenly, something slithered up behind Mrs. Bleeblebrom.

CHAPTER 8

A Past Conflict Revealed

"Having fun loafing around, Mrs. Bleeble-BROOM?!" Principal Cranklebucket snipped.

Mrs. Bleeblebrom jumped, spilling coffee all down the front of Mr. Gutsucker's shirt. "Ahhh!" he screamed. "That's really hot!"

A little bit splashed on me, too. "Eeep!" I yelped, then slapped a hand over my mouth and bit my lip.

"What was that?" Mrs. Bleeblebrom asked.

"A mouse?" Mr. Gutsucker offered.

Cranklebucket was furious. "Would you two stop goofing off and get back to..."

Mrs. Bleeblebrom interrupted him sharply, "Look, Ray, my children are at recess and..."

"Then you need to get back to your classroom and prepare for your next lesson! Get back to work! Move it!"

His screaming blew Mrs. Bleeblebrom's hair back, but Mr. Gutsucker was bald, so nothing happened to him.

Principal Cranklebucket sluthered from the room and the door slammed behind him though he hadn't even touched it.

"Gosh," Mr. Gutsucker said, still wiping coffee from his shirt with a handful of napkins. "Why is that guy so mean to you?"

Mrs. Bleeblebrom sighed deeply. "Ray Cranklebucket and I have known each other for a long, long time. We went to college together. I first saw him in a writing class I took in my second year. He was wearing a hat, raincoat and boots. All black. Always dripping wet though it hadn't rained for days."

"That's odd. And what's weirder is that he's still like that."

"Yes, I know. Our class had an excellent teacher

named Nathan Goodlang. And near the end of the semester, Professor Goodlang held a story writing contest. Whoever won got to write another story and have it placed in the school library. Then they'd be rich and famous from that day on."

"Wow, what happened?"

"The day arrived when all the stories were read out loud in class. When I finished reading my story, *The Cow With the Udder Named Blubber*, Cranklebucket yelled, 'Ha! That's the worst story I've ever heard!'"

"So you lost?"

"No, I won. Professor Goodlang told the class *The Cow With the Udder Named Blubber* was the best story he'd ever heard! Ray's story, *Little Peeps Pops When He Poops* came in last."

"I'll bet he was really mad," Mr. Gutsucker said.

"Yes, very, very mad. And ever since that day, he's never liked me. That's why he's having our class do the school play this year."

"It is?"

"Yes, because he thinks we will fail. And when

we fail, I will lose my job. That's his plan. He told me so himself in a note."

"That's terrible!"

"I know. But I've thought about it, and even though Reeker smells and Clara talks in animal noises and Clay always has to rhyme and one child has green skin with polka dots, and we have a girl who can't go anywhere without that ant-eater, I believe in our class. I believe we can do it."

We sure can Mrs. Bleeblebrom, I thought.

Then I heard Mrs. Bleeblebrom set down her coffee cup and prepare to leave.

"Hey, I almost forgot," Mr. Gutsucker said. "What story did you write for the library? And if you got so rich and famous, what are you doing here?"

"Well, I worked hard and wrote my story, but I only had one copy of it. On the day I was supposed to turn it in to the library, I couldn't find it anywhere. It just disappeared."

"That's terrible!"

"Well, yes. But that was a long time ago."

I listened a little longer, then snuck back into

the nurse's office to check on Chunky.

I found her still moaning and laying on her back with her eyes closed. I decided to let her sleep, then ran to class before Mrs. Bleeblebrom knew I was missing.

* * *

I have no idea what Mrs. Bleeblebrom taught us that afternoon. I couldn't stop thinking about that mean Principal Cranklebucket, and how bad he was to my teacher, and how afraid I was of him.

Chunky came back to class eventually. She was bandaged around the head but was otherwise in good spirits, as always.

"Look at my pretty pink bandage!" she told me excitedly.

It was pink all right. Bright pink.

"Uh, it's nice," I squeaked out.

"Glad you like it!" she chirped.

I didn't feel so good just then. My stomach was all churned up from so much worrying.

After school that day I told Mrs. Bleeblebrom I was just too scared to write the play. "I'm scared I'll write a bad play and the other kids will laugh at me and not want to be my friend anymore," I told her. "And I'm scared of that mean old Principal Cranklebucket!"

Mrs. Bleeblebrom looked me straight in the eyes. "Ayla, I'm going to tell you something even scarier than that."

"What?"

"Some people go their whole lives without discovering their talents, because they're too afraid to try anything."

"That's not scary," I told her. "Messing up is scary."

"Ayla, everything good in this life comes at a risk. You might not succeed at what you try, but believe it or not, sometimes you can learn more when you fail than when you succeed."

"Really?"

"Really. A failure today might actually help you succeed in the future, and succeed bigger and better

61

than you ever imagined, if you allow yourself to learn from your mistakes. Now, I want you to go home and write the best play for the class you possibly can. I know you can do it and I'll help you. Do you think you can have it ready by Monday?"

"Well, I'll try Mrs. Bleeblebrom, I really will. I'm scared, but I'll try."

"You'll do fine. I have faith in you."

"Mrs. Bleeblebrom?"

"Yes?"

"I'm really glad you're my teacher."

"So am I, Ayla. So am I."

* * *

I worked hard all that week and wrote my play. I even worked through the weekend.

The only time I stopped was when Emmitt and Nolan came by one afternoon to play. They wanted to play 'Stick It To the Man,' Emmitt's favorite game.

Each person has a stick or a small branch and you run around trying to knock the stick out of the other person's hand, kind of like a sword battle. If you knock it from their hand, you get a point. Then it starts all over again.

We went to the back yard to choose our sticks. We battled for only ten seconds when I knocked Emmitt's stick from his hand. I yelled "Stick it to the man!" and *WHACK,* smacked him on the back of his leg.

"Owww!" he yelped. "You're not supposed to do that!"

"Ha ha!" I answered.

After a couple hours, I told the boys I had to go in the house to work on my play.

As Nolan was leaving, I asked him, "Why were you guys following Principal Cranklebucket in the parking lot at school the other day?"

"We followed him home," Nolan said. "We found out he lives at the zoo."

"Really? At the *zoo*? How strange."

"We thought so too," he said, then Emmitt blared his truck horn and poked his head out the window. "Come on, Nolan! Let's go!

"Well, gotta go. See you later, Ayla."

"Bye, Nolan. Bye, Emmitt!" I yelled and waved at them from the door.

I pulled my play from my bookbag and got to work. I couldn't wait to get to school Monday and show the class!

CHAPTER 9

Caught!

On Monday morning, I ran to school as fast as I could.

I was so excited!

Mrs. Bleeblebrom began the class. "Ok, Ayla, would you please tell the class the name of your play?"

"Gladly," I said. "It's called, *Cranky Duck and the Orangutan from Outer Space*."

"Awesome!" Chunky yelled.

"Dang!" Jimmy sulked.

"*BAAAAAAHHH*!" Clara yelled, just because she felt like it.

"Smoke 'em if ya got 'em," Reeker said, which drew a sideways look from Mrs. Bleeblebrom.

"Lrig og uoy!" Bob yelled, but no one

understood.

"Ok," Mrs. Bleeblebrom said, "Now we *all* have some work to do. Let's see, hmmm," she looked around the class. "You know what? This will be hard enough without everyone having to learn their lines by heart, so on the night of the play we'll write each of your lines on a tiny piece of paper and tape it to your sleeves."

"Good idea!" everyone agreed.

"Now let's get practicing."

* * *

On the evening of the play, I was excited and nervous at the same time.

I entered the classroom as some of the other kids shuffled in. It was then I noticed Mrs. Bleeblebrom looked very worried.

"Children, please sit down," she told us. She looked at me. "Ayla, I'm afraid I have bad news."

"What?"

"Well, I had your play in my desk, but now it's

gone! I can't find it anywhere! I feel awful!" She slumped at her desk and put her head in her big glove-hands.

I looked around frantically. "But I don't have any other copies!"

"Oh, no," someone said.

"Holy noodle strainer!" someone else said.

"Now we won't be able to tape the lines to the kids' sleeves!" Mrs. Bleeblebrom exclaimed. "I need a drink of water."

She covered her face with her big hands and left the room.

I sat at my desk trying to breathe normal as my heart raced a million beats per second. At that moment I knew it was all up to me.

The moment of truth. Do or die.

I wrote something on my desk, then walked to the front of the room and stood up tall on a chair. "I'm going to tell you all something no one else knows," I said as the words W E C A N D O T H I S appeared in giant letters on the board behind me. "If we fail at this play, Mrs. Bleeblebrom will lose her job."

"No!" the kids yelled.

"Yes, it's true," I assured them. "You don't want that, and I don't want that. And Mrs. Bleeblebrom certainly doesn't want that. So if we're going to do this play tonight, then you'll just have to do it from memory."

"Oh, no!" someone screamed.

"Are you sure?" someone else screamed.

Mrs. Bleeblebrom came back into the room with her glass of water, looked at what I had written on the board, tried to smile but instead slumped again at her desk.

"Look, do the best you can," I told the class. "We have no other choice. So who's with me? Who's going to do this for Mrs. Bleeblebrom?"

"Don't worry Mrs. B.," Clay yelled. "We can do this, you'll see!"

"Yeah!" everyone cheered loudly.

The ant-eater waved its nose in the air with glee.

Mrs. Bleeblebrom stood up, reinvigorated by

the encouragement. "Ok, everyone," she clapped, "Start getting into your costumes."

I looked over at the ant-eater, and that's when it hit me.

Not the ant-eater, but a thought.

"Of course!" I yelled out loud. I remembered something I overhead in the teachers' lounge the day Chunky got hurt. "I'll be right back," I said, and jumped from the chair and headed for the door.

"How long will you be gone?" Mrs. Bleeblebrom asked nervously.

"I'm not sure," was all I could say. "Hopefully not long."

I left the room and ran to find the Bunson twins. They were on the playground.

"Emmitt! Nolan! Get your trucks. We have to go!"

* * *

The truck tires squealed as we shot out of the school parking lot.

"Where're we going?" Nolan yelled over the wind from our open windows as we raced down the highway.

"You'll see," I yelled back. "Turn on your lights, it's getting dark."

Emmitt was right behind us in his truck.

"Turn here," I told Nolan.

"Here?"

"Yes, here!"

We pulled into the zoo parking lot, and just as we did, I thought I saw a dark shape near the front gate.

"Look! There's Principal Cranklebucket!"

"I see him!" Emmitt exclaimed.

We jumped out of the trucks and took off running. The shape turned and looked back for a second before bolting through the zoo entrance.

"Now *he* sees *us*!" I revealed, trying to keep up with the twins.

We chased through the front gate, trying to keep our principal in our sights.

"Don't lose him!" I yelled to Emmitt and Nolan,

a few steps behind them.

We ran past the duck pond that greets visitors when they enter the zoo. It's one of my favorite features of the park. You know, I have to say, I really love the zo...

"Watch out for that goose!" Emmitt called out.

"I see him!" I jumped over it with a bounding leap.

We saw Principal Cranklebucket run toward the reptile house. It was becoming so dark it was hard to see him.

"Don't lose him," I cautioned.

We neared the reptile house to find a sidewalk full of snakes and alligators!

Cranklebucket had let them out.

"Watch out!" I screamed to the twins.

Emmitt and Nolan kicked snakes out of their way, left and right. Suddenly, an alligator ran towards them, snapping its jaws, ready to chomp down on them.

Without warning, a snake fell from a tree and landed on Nolan. Emmitt grabbed the snake. "This should come in handy!" he said and jumped on the back of the alligator and tied its mouth shut with the snake.

"Good going!" Nolan told him.

We finally got through the snakes and alligators, but now a group of emperor penguins littered the walkway next to the Antarctica exhibit.

"Excuse me! Sorry!" Nolan said, dodging penguins left and right.

"Look! Cranklebucket is headed toward the gorilla exhibit!" I blurted, breathing heavily.

We got through the penguins unscathed, but as we passed Australia Land, two kangaroos jumped onto the path. One of them punched Emmitt in the stomach and he fell to the path in a heap. The other kicked Nolan's legs out from under him, sending him flying into a fountain.

KER-SPLASH!

"Emmitt! Nolan!"

I couldn't believe what was happening.

Emmitt got up, a little dazed, and pretty mad.

"Come here, you!" Emmitt shouted and

grabbed the kangaroo from behind. "You'll come in handy!"

Nolan jumped out of the fountain.

"Nolan! Grab that one!" Emmitt told him.

They ran, each with a kangaroo tucked under his arm. I trailed several steps behind them.

We came to the entrance of the gorilla exhibit and I shook the gate. "It's locked!"

"Stand back, Ayla," Emmitt informed.

I backed up just as Emmitt and Nolan pressed their kangaroos against the gate. The kangaroos kicked and punched, and punched and kicked!

BANG! BANG! BANG! BANG!

Soon the gate came crashing down.

"Yea!" I screamed.

The twins tossed the kangaroos aside and they scampered away.

"Follow me!" I ordered.

We ran through the gate.

* * *

Back at the school, it was nearing time for the play to start. Mrs. Bleeblebrom shuffled the kids to the backstage area of the auditorium.

Hundreds and hundreds of people jammed into the seats. A packed house! You might think this was good, but it wasn't. Word had gotten out that the play would be a disaster, so everyone in town came out to see it flop.

Mrs. Bleeblebrom peeked her head out of the curtain and looked around. *Where's Ayla?* she thought worriedly.

* * *

Back at the zoo, Emmitt, Nolan and I ran to a hut next to the gorilla cage. We found the door unlocked.

Nolan opened it slowly. It creaked a bit, making me jump.

"Shhhhhh!" Emmitt shushed from behind me.

"There's no one in here," Nolan whispered in front of me.

74

We went in.

The hut was dark, except for a little reading lamp on a cluttered desk by the far wall. A large window to the right looked out on the gorilla cage. Papers and books were piled high on the desk. I ran over and hurriedly shuffled through the papers, not caring that pens, pencils and books fell to the floor in a mess.

It's got to be here somewhere! I thought.

I picked up a thick set of papers. The first page read '*Chumley Crumples while Chewing Chocolate Chihuahuas,* By: Ray Cranklebucket.' I threw that down and picked up another: '*Billy the Ugly Platypus Finally Finds a Wife,* By: Ray Cranklebucket.'

"Ayla, what are you doing?" Nolan whispered tensely.

"Yes, Ayla. What *are* you doing?" came a very loud, very deep voice at the door.

CHAPTER 10

The Show Must Go On!

We spun around and gasped.

Principal Cranklebucket had blocked the way out!

I felt my legs shake. I backed up against the desk knocking more papers to the ground. Then I saw something out of the corner of my eye.

"I knew it!" I said, suddenly feeling very bold.

I bent over and picked up *Cranky Duck and the Orangutan from Outer Space*. However, 'By: Ayla Bayla' had been erased and instead it read, 'By: Ray Cranklebucket.'

"You stole my play! You spied on us, didn't you? You knew those kids might not do the play if they had to do it from memory."

"That's correct," Cranklebucket slithered and sluthered his way through the door, coming nearer to us. "According to my watch, the play is supposed to start right about…now! But you are here, and the play is here. So the show will be cancelled for sure. Ha Ha Ha Ha! Get comfortable, we're going NOWHERE!"

* * *

The crowd grew louder and louder.

"We Want The Play! We Want The Play!"

Mrs. Bleeblebrom poked her head through the curtain at stage left. With a look of terror, she scanned the crowd for any sign that I had come back.

Where is she?

The crowd began chanting "Ayla Bayla! We want the play-a! Ayla Bayla! We want the play-a!"

This is getting ugly…

Mrs. Bleeblebrom pulled her head from the curtain, took a step backward without looking, and tripped right over Reeker McBean.

"Ow!" he squealed.

The smell of roasted marshmallows wafted up right before my teacher slammed hard onto the floor. *Wham!*

* * *

I yelled at Principal Cranklebucket, "You're wrong! The play won't be cancelled! The kids are going to do the play anyway, from memory if they have to!"

I screamed as loud as I could so maybe someone, or something, *anything*, outside would hear me. Getting angrier, I spat out, "You won't get away with this! You aren't going to get Mrs. Bleeblebrom fired as you hoped!"

"Really?" Principal Cranklebucket mocked, locking the door. "We'll just see about that!"

He slithered and sluthered along the far wall of the hut, still dripping wet though it wasn't raining. "You know, Miss Bayla, the best writer in this school is not you, nor is it Mrs. Bleeble-BROOM. It's me! Do you understand? I'm the greatest story writer EVER!"

A deafening thunderclap crashed outside, though there was not a cloud in the sky.

I looked beneath the gorilla observation window. A tiny opening near the floor caught my eye. Emmitt looked that way too, but noticed something different. Our eyes met, and we nodded.

Emmitt took off full speed across the room and slammed into Principal Cranklebucket with a full football block. The dripping man slammed into the observation window with a loud *THUD!*

That very same instant, a huge, hairy arm shot through the opening near the floor and grabbed Principal Cranklebucket by the leg.

"Aaaaahhhhhhhhhhh!" Principal Cranklebucket roared, "Help me!"

"Oh, we'll help you alright," Nolan said as he grabbed some rope. The twins dove on top of him.

They wrestled with arms and legs and gorilla limbs going in every direction! The squeak and squeal of rope on wet rubber was so loud I had to cover my ears.

With Principal Cranklebucket soon tied up

securely, including his mouth, I said, "Hurry! We have no time to waste!"

I grabbed my play from the desk as the boys picked up our struggling principal. We ran through the zoo and out into the parking lot. Penguins, snakes, geese, flamingos, ostriches and kangaroos fled the zoo in all directions.

We tossed our principal into Emmitt's truck. I hurriedly grabbed Nolan's keys and said, "Nolan, you go with Emmitt. I don't know what to do with Cranklebucket, so you guys figure that out. I'll take your truck and get my play back to the school as fast as possible."

I jammed the pedal to the floor, squealed the tires, and left the zoo in a trail of gravel, smoke and bird feathers.

* * *

"Mrs. B! Mrs. B!"

My beloved teacher was sprawled out on the floor, not quite hearing me. I stooped over her and waved papers in her face to give her air.

"Mrs. Bleeblebrom, wake up! I've got the play, we can pin the lines to the kids sleeves now."

She shot right up. "Not now, we have no time. You have to get out there. We have to start!"

"But Mrs. Bleeblebrom, I have to tell you something."

"Not now. Later."

She shoved me through the curtain. The roar of the cheering crowd hit me in the face like a ton of bricks.

The house lights dimmed, and just before the spotlight hit me, I thought I saw Emmitt and Nolan leaning against the back wall with the dark shape of Principal Cranklebucket propped up between them.

And how'd that gorilla get in here?

CHAPTER 11

"It's Not Fair!"

It turns out everyone hit their lines perfectly, and at the end of the play, the whole audience stood and cheered. "Bravo! Bravo!"

I went out to take a final bow and the crowd was so loud it hurt my ears. They even threw flowers on the stage, which I quickly grabbed up because Reeker, who stood beside me, was trying to eat them.

I thought I smelled rotten eggs.

"Great job, Ayla!" Mrs. Bleeblebrom congratulated as I walked off the stage.

"Thanks," I replied. "Mrs. Bleeblebrom, I really have to tell you something. Something important."

"Not now Ayla," she said. "Whatever it is, you

can tell me tomorrow. Right now, the entire audience is waiting in the hallway. Your public is dying to meet you."

* * *

The next day, when the last child left the classroom for recess, Mrs. Bleeblebrom said, "Ok, Ayla, what did you want to tell me last night? And I hope it has something to do with why Emmitt, Nolan, and a gorilla," she made a weird face, "had Principal Cranklebucket tied up and propped against the back wall."

"Well," I told her, "when my play turned up missing on the day of the performance, it made me think of something you said the other day."

"What was that?" Mrs. Bleeblebrom asked.

"Well, first I have to tell you something. Promise you won't get mad?"

"Hmmmm," is all she said.

"Well, I accidentally overheard you talking to Mr. Gutsucker in the teachers' lounge the other day."

"You did?"

"Yes, but I didn't mean to! It was an accident! Chunky was hit in the head, and all I wanted was a Tootsie Roll, and…"

Mrs. Bleeblebrom smirked. "So what did you hear?"

"Remember when Mr. Gutsucker asked you why you weren't rich and famous for having your prize winning story in the college library, and you said it turned up missing?"

"Yes, I remember."

"Well, I thought about that and about how much Principal Cranklebucket doesn't like you and the fact that he wanted you to lose your job if the play went badly, or if it didn't happen at all, and…"

Mrs. Bleeblebrom's face suddenly lit up like a lightbulb. "You don't mean…?"

"Yes! Principal Cranklebucket stole my play. And I think he has your story, too."

"My goodness!"

"What's the title of your story, Mrs. Bleeblebrom?"

"It's called, *Billy the Ugly Platypus*…"

"…*Finally Finds a Wife*. Yes, I know. I saw it. But it had Principal Cranklebucket's name on it, not yours."

"Oh, so he put his name on it so he could be rich and famous? That was a rotten thing to do!"

"But now we know where it is, so we can go get it and get him in trouble and…"

"No," Mrs. Bleeblebrom said flatly, holding up a glove-hand. "No, I don't want to do that."

"Why not?" I screeched. "It's not fair! It's not his story. Don't you want to become rich and famous?"

"In a way, Ayla, I already am rich and famous. Not because I have a lot of money, or because I have a book in the library. It's because of you."

"Me?"

"Yes, you. You and all the children I've ever taught. For example, what about the play you wrote? If I didn't encourage you to write that play, you never would've done it, right?"

"Yeah, I guess you're right."

"And now you know you have a talent for writing. And for the rest of your life, every time you think you can't do something, you'll look back on this time—and how you overcame your fear and wrote that play—and things might just be a little easier."

"I never thought of that," I said.

"You know, Ayla," Mrs. Bleeblebrom put a glove-hand on my shoulder, "you are rich, too."

"I am?"

"Yes, you have a lot of friends. And when you help them and allow them to help you, it makes your life rich, richer than anything money can buy."

"You know Mrs. Bleeblebrom, you're pretty smart...for a teacher," I smiled.

"Thanks Ayla, you're pretty smart, too. By the way, you'll need to go to the gymnasium tomorrow after lunch."

"Am I in trouble?"

"You'll see."

CHAPTER 12

Unexpected Honor

After lunch the next day, I played a game of tetherball on the playground with Chunky and Jimmy before I was supposed to go to the gym.

"I think I'm in big trouble," I told them, then I thought about what Mrs. Bleeblebrom said about allowing my friends to help me when I needed it. "Hey, will you guys go with me to the gym?"

"Sure!" Chunky said, and I thought I saw her sneak a wink at Jimmy.

We entered the school, but everyone was gone. The hallways were empty. "What's going on?" I asked, a little scared.

We turned the corner and entered the gym. It was packed with all the teachers, students and parents from the school.

"There she is!" a boy yelled, and everyone cheered with a loud roar. They stood and clapped and stomped their feet.

"AY-LA! AY-LA! AY-LA!"

Jimmy and Chunky walked me to a little stage in the middle of the gym. Mrs. Bleeblebrom was there with the woman who runs the library. And...the mayor?

Yes, the mayor!

Mayor Scandal stepped up to the microphone. "Please, everyone! Please, quiet down."

Shushes peppered the crowd.

"It has come to my attention that a little girl named Ayla Bayla has written the best play this town has ever seen. So on behalf of the city, I would like to give Ayla this award."

Mayor Scandal handed me a giant, golden pencil, two feet long. It was so heavy I could hardly lift it!

"And that's not all," he continued. "I would like to introduce our town's head librarian, Miss Stacie

Julio."

People clapped and cheered.

"On behalf of the town library," Miss Julio said, "I want to give this to Ayla Bayla," and she handed me a book. "I'm pleased to announce that *Cranky Duck and the Orangutan from Outer Space* will now be in the library for everyone to read."

The book was my play, and it had my name on it and everything! I lifted it high above my head to show the crowd.

Everyone stood and cheered. It was very loud.

I looked over at Mrs. Bleeblebrom. A tear ran down her cheek. I smiled at her.

When everyone finally quieted down, I stepped to the microphone and said, "This is for Mrs. Bleeblebrom. The best teacher ever!" and the crowd stood and cheered. But something strange was happening by the side door. People were looking and pointing and whispering.

Something, or someone, was shuffling through the door.

CHAPTER 13

A Change of Heart

Principal Cranklebucket!

In a suit?

In a peach-colored suit?

He shuffled to the stage, stepped up, and tripped and fell flat on his face in front of the mayor. The mayor kindly helped him up amidst a smattering of giggles and whispers.

Then the place was silent.

Dead silent.

Except for a baby crying in the back.

Principal Cranklebucket stepped to the microphone and said, "I haven't been very kind to Ayla Bayla…"

The crowd showered him with boos.

"And I especially haven't been kind to Mrs. Bleeble-Broom, er—I mean, Mrs. Bleeble*brom*."

More boos.

"And for all that, I am very sorry."

Silence.

"I stole Ayla's play," he blubbered, and the booing began again, "because it was better than anything I'd ever read. I was so jealous, I wanted it for myself."

The boos got even louder.

"But thanks to two young men named Emmitt and Nolan, and one very feisty gorilla, I watched the play and enjoyed it very much."

The booing stopped.

"I saw how much other people enjoyed it, and then it occurred to me..." He took a step back and nearly fell again. His bottom lip quivered a little as a single tear rolled down his cheek. He stepped back up to the microphone. "...that because of what I did, you all almost didn't get to see Ayla's excellent play."

At that moment, I noticed he wasn't dripping wet anymore, except for the single tear on his cheek.

"How could I have been so selfish?" he bellowed.

A gorilla in the back row sobbed loudly.

"I used to think that if I wasn't the best, then I was nothing. So I had to steal other people's talent, like yours Mrs. Bleeblebrom." He looked down and took a deep breath, "The truth is, when Mrs. Bleeblebrom and I were in college together, her story, *The Cow With the Udder Named Blubber*, was the greatest story I'd ever heard. The other students loved it. Even our teacher loved it, Mr. Nathan Goodlang, whom I've invited here today. Please stand up Mr. Goodlang."

The teacher stood and gave a little wave. The people cheered, especially Mrs. Bleeblebrom.

Principal Cranklebucket looked at my teacher, "I couldn't stand knowing you were a better writer than me, but you are. I've done a lot of things wrong, and hurt a lot of people, including you. So I ask that you'd forgive me."

She nodded at him with a big smile. People clapped and cheered.

He continued, "After seeing Ayla's play, I realized that I could enjoy her talent and be happy for her, that I *should* be happy for her, and can still be happy with myself. I should be grateful for who I am and what I can do, which is to try to be the best school principal I can be, even if I'm not the best one that ever was."

The crowd clapped and cheered!

"But that's not all. I want to do my best to make things right. That's why I wanted to give this to the library." He handed a book to Miss Julio. She looked at it and held it high over her head for everyone to see: *Billy the Ugly Platypus Finally Finds a Wife,* By: Jennica Bleeblebrom.

The crowd cheered!

I cheered!

The gorilla cheered!

I ran over and hugged Principal Cranklebucket and told him, "Thanks P.C.! You're a good man and a great principal. You can hang out in our classroom anytime."

"Thanks, Ayla," he said. "Ayla Bayla."

Look for the Second Book in
The Ayla Bayla Book Collection:

Reeker McBean

Saves

Christmas

By David Harold

Available Now!

The following is an excerpt from:

Reeker McBean Saves Christmas

Chapter 1

Smothered in a lime-green bean-bag chair his father recently rescued from an ex-hippy's garage sale, Reeker McBean stared at the blank TV screen and thought: *What's going to happen now...am I going to die?*

It was a very real question. A difficult one. One that needed an answer.

Reeker McBean wasn't exactly a barrel of confidence. He wasn't even a pickle jar of confidence when it comes down to it. In fact, he lacked the confidence to feel adequate for even the smallest and most mundane of tasks in life.

Reeker McBean wasn't particularly well liked at school, save for a couple of troublemakers who needed a henchman—or a scapegoat—for their fledgling exploits in delinquency.

Chumps, Reeker thought.

But he needed the chumps as much as they needed him. They were his only connection beyond his fake world of video games and cartoons.

Some people really liked living in such fake worlds.

Reeker did not.

He hated it.

Deep down he craved adventure, but was simply too afraid to do anything about it.

Squirming in his big, lime-green bean-bag chair, he picked a booger from his nose and rolled it into a tight ball. He rubbed it deep into the fibers of his brown Toughskin pants and slumped further in the chair as despair etched its way across his face like the granite of Mount Rushmore.

Yes, Reeker McBean was simply afraid of life.

Suddenly, a different sort of emotion coursed through his slight frame, sending a shiver up his spine.

No wait...it was just fear. Again.

Of course.

But this time fear gripped him in a brand new way for a brand new reason. It was brought on from thinking about what happened earlier in the day.

What happened earlier in the day puzzled him. An awful, nuzzling, kuzzling, puzzle.

He looked down at the snot smudged into his pants and thought, *Mom is going to kill me when she sees this!*

And he was right. She would.

He quickly wiped his shirt-sleeve on his pants in an attempt to erase the crime.

"Reeker!" a voice screeched from the dining room, "What are you doing in there?"

"I don't nose!" Reeker shouted to his mother. "Nothing!"

Did he say 'nose'? his mother thought with a shake of her head. No, he couldn't have.

Available Now – By David Harold:

Reeker McBean
Saves
Christmas

About the Author

David Harold is an international journalist who travels the globe in search of outlandish characters and situations to feed the toxic pool of his bizarre imagination. When in the USA, he divides his time between Colorado, Florida and the Great State of Ohio.

The Ayla Bayla Book Collection

Available Now:
Ayla Bayla
Reeker McBean Saves Christmas

Coming Soon:
Ayla Bayla: Hangman's Hill
Clara Bell's Intensely Amazing African Adventure

Schwierd Books
www.schwierdbooks.com

072814

Thank You

If this book succeeds at all, everything can be owed to one person: My friend Pam Sibert-Hooker.

In the initial stages of this book, many people read, reviewed, edited and voiced a wide range of opinions about the story. But Pam believed in the project (and me) so much that she actually used her valuable time to tirelessly work *for years* on behalf of seeing this book through to production, and keeping me sane and off the ledge in the process. I would have given up long ago if not for her faith, excitement, encouragement and belief in these stories, and in me as a writer. And for that, Pam, I can never thank you enough.

A great friend and skilled journalist, Amy Keller was the first person to see this story. She didn't know it at the time, but my career as an author literally rested in her hands. A bad report, and I was probably through. But not only did she enjoy the story and take it across the country to show her nephew, she encouraged me to continue it as a series. And thus, the Ayla Bayla series of books was born. Amy—you've been an invaluable person in my life. Without your initial encouragement, none of this would have ever happened.

- David Harold

18008280R00065

Made in the USA
San Bernardino, CA
23 December 2014